A CAT IN THE HAT STORY

CAT OUT OF WATER

This is a work of fiction. Names, characters, places, and incidents either are the product of the author's imagination or are used fictitiously. Any resemblance to actual persons, living or dead, events, or locales is entirely coincidental.

 Published in the United States by RH Graphic, an imprint of Random House Children's Books, a division of Penguin Random House LLC, New York.

RH Graphic with the book design is a trademark of Penguin Random House LLC.

Visit us on the Web!
Seussville.com
RHKidsGraphic.com
@RHKidsGraphic

Educators and librarians, for a variety of teaching tools, visit us at RHTeachersLibrarians.com

Library of Congress Cataloging-in-Publication Data is available upon request.
ISBN 978-0-593-70303-8 (trade)
ISBN 978-0-593-70304-5 (lib. bdg.)
ISBN 978-0-593-70305-2 (ebook)

Editor: Whitney Leopard
Designer: Bob Bianchini
Copy Editor: Stephanie Bay
Managing Editor: Katy Miller
Production Manager: Jen Jie Li

Printed in Canada
10 9 8 7 6 5 4 3 2 1
First Edition

A comic on every bookshelf

A CAT IN THE HAT STORY

CAT OUT OF WATER

Art Baltazar

RH GRAPHIC
NEW YORK

Dedicated to my family:
my lovely wife, Rose, and my kids,
Audrey, Gordy, and Sonny. Without
them, I wouldn't be a cool CAT
with a cartoonist's HAT.

IS IT ALMOST FINISHED?
IN A MINUTE.
JUST FILLING UP THE BOWL.

POUR

THERE YOU GO! ALL CLEAN AND READY.

NOTHING BEATS A CLEAN AND FRESH FISHBOWL.
JUMP

WHAT A PERFECT DAY.
AH.
THIS IS THE LIFE.
NOTHING CAN RUIN THIS PERFECT MOMENT...
WELL, EXCEPT IF...

...YOU-KNOW-WHO SHOWS UP.

THE CAT?
SSHH...

...WE DON'T NEED ANY OF HIS SHENANIGANS TODAY.

KNOCK KNOCK
KNOCK
OH, NO.

HE'S HERE.

WHO'S HERE?
IT'S THE CAT.
ARE YOU SURE?

WE GOTTA CHECK AND SEE.

WAIT!
DON'T OPEN THE DOOR!
TURN OFF THE LIGHTS!
MAYBE HE'LL GO AWAY!

CLICK

CLICK

PEEK

the CAT IN THE HAT
IN
CAT OUT OF WATER
GUEST STARRING...
THING 1 & THING 2
WELCOME
BY ART BALTAZAR

HI, KIDS!

HI, CAT!
I SEE YOU!

YOU WEREN'T SUPPOSED TO SAY HI BACK!
HEE HEE.
HA HA.

WHY'D YOU TURN OFF THE LIGHTS?

SO, UH...
WHAT ARE YOU DOING IN THERE TODAY?

UM...
NOTHING.

FISH SAID NOT TO LET YOU IN THE HOUSE.

HMM.
NOW WHY WOULD HE SAY THAT?

I THINK IT'S BECAUSE YOU LEFT A BIG MESS LAST TIME YOU CAME OVER.

YEAH, YEAH.
GOOD, GOOD.

REALLY?

OKAY.
HOW ABOUT THIS?
WE

WHAT IF THIS TIME, I DON'T MAKE A MESS?
THIS WAY WE CAN STILL HAVE FUN!

WITH US?

YEAH.
WE CAN HANG OUT TOGETHER.
I DON'T KNOW...

C'MON, IT'LL BE FUN.

NO, NO, NO!

SO, NO HOT-AIR BALLOONS THAT POP INTO GLITTER?
BUT THE SPARKLES!

AND NO RAINBOW GOOP THAT STAINS OUR MOM'S CHAIR?
IF YOU INSIST. NO MESS.
CROSS MY HEART.

OKAY.
TURN

OPEN
UGH.
WHY...WHY?
OH, WHY?

FIRST THINGS FIRST...
...LET THERE BE LIGHT!
WELC

CLICK

CLICK

HELLO, FISH.
HEY.

HMM. ONE WONDERS...
WHO WONDERS?

...HOW CAN YOU HAVE FUN IN SUCH A SMALL BOWL?
I'M FINE, CAT.
HOW CAN WE HANG OUT IF THERE IS NO ROOM?
THAT'S NOT...

WHAT IF YOU HAD A MUCH BIGGER PLACE?
ONE THAT FITS ALL OF US?
OH, PLEASE.
DON'T GET ANY IDEAS.

YES! YES!
WHAT IF WE ALL PRETENDED TO BE IN A BIGGER BOWL TOGETHER?!
UM... NO THANKS.
THIS BOWL IS THE PERFECT SIZE.

WAIT!

WHAT IF WE ALL PRETENDED TO BE FISH, TOO?!

Y'KNOW!
IT WILL BE GOOD TO STRETCH YOUR LEGS!
I DON'T HAVE LEGS.
MAYBE YOU WOULDN'T BE SO GRUMPY.

YOU JUST MIGHT BE HAPPY TO SEE ME.
YOU'RE DREAMING.

WAIT, CAT...
YOU SAID YOU WERE GOING TO BEHAVE.
I'M NOT SURE I LIKE WHERE THIS IS GOING.

BAMP!

THAT'S TRUE.
THERE'S JUST ONE THING...

...FISH DIDN'T SAY NO TO A BIGGER BOWL!
LET'S DO THIS!

BE RIGHT BACK!
SWOOSH!
UGH.

SEE?
I'M BACK!
GREAT.

LOOKEE HERE!
IS THAT A SHOEBOX?
EVEN BETTER.

A THING BOX!
1
2

MEET
THING
1...
AND
THING
2!
WE REALLY
DON'T NEED THIS
RIGHT NOW.

CHEER UP, BUDDY!
WHAT BETTER WAY TO MAKE A BIGGER FISHBOWL THAN WITH THE HELP OF MORE FRIENDS?
I HAVE ENOUGH FRIENDS.

OOF!
DROP!

OH, NO.
I'M AFRAID OF WHAT IS ABOUT TO HAPPEN.

OH, DON'T WORRY.
HA HA!
I MUST ADMIT...
...THING 1 AND THING 2 MAY GET OUT OF CONTROL SOMETIMES.
IT'S NOT THEM, CAT.
IT'S YOU.

LET'S GET THIS PARTY STARTED!
PARTY?

FWOOSH
SWOOSH

UM...
MAYBE WE
SHOULD...
YEAH,
YEAH.
YOU GO
THAT WAY...
...I'LL GO
THE OTHER.

RUN
RUN
RUN

RUN
RUN
RUN

TURN
TURN ON

PSSH!

TURN
TURN OFF

WHEW!

RUN
RUN

TURN ON
PSSHH!!
TURN

GO, THING 1!
GO, GO, THING 2!
DRIP
SPLASH
SPLASH
DRIP
SPLASH
SPLASH
NO! NO!
TURN IT ALL OFF!

SWOOSH!
SWOOSH!
SWOOSH!

FSSSHH

TURN OFF

HUFF
HUFF
I CAN'T KEEP UP.
THING 1 IS TOO FAST.
HUFF
HUFF
THING 2 IS FASTER.
I'M EXHAUSTED.

TURN ON
PPSSSHH

TWIST ON
PSSHH

TURN ON
PPSSH

TWIST ON
PSSH

TURN ON
PSSHH

SQUEAK
TURN
TURN

FLIP

OOH. MORE WATER!
PPSSSHH
HOW REFRESHING!

PSSHHH
BLUB
BLUB

SPLASH
SPA-LASH
-LASH

PSSSH

BUMP
1
2

RRR
RUMBLE
SPLISH
SPLISH
SPLISH

WAIT!
DON'T OPEN!

TURN

SPWOOSH!

I MUST ADMIT...
PSSH
PSSH

...THIS ISN'T QUITE WHAT I THOUGHT A BIGGER BOWL WOULD LOOK LIKE...
PSSH
PSSH

...BUT THIS WILL WORK OUT PERFECTLY!
PSSH

SEE?
WHAT DO YOU THINK?
NOW WE CAN ALL HANG OUT TOGETHER AND HAVE SOME FUN!
SWIM
SPLISH

GASP!
IT IS LIKE WE'RE A FISH FAMILY!

BLOOP

SEE?
NOW WE CAN SWIM TOGETHER!

I THOUGHT CATS HATE WATER.
HA!
I LOVE IT!

AND SO DO THE KIDS.

HA HA!
SPLASH
SPLASH
THIS IS JUST LIKE A SWIMMING POOL!
SPLASH

SEE?
NOW WATCH THIS.

JUMP
LEAP

CANNONBALL
SPLASH

WATCH OUT!
AAH!

SPLASH
1
2

I SCORE YOU A TEN.
10
1
2

HOORAY!
PERFECT DIVE!
1
2

YOU KNOW WHAT CAN MAKE THIS EVEN BETTER?

LEAP

THROW
INFLATABLES!
THROW
TOSS
TOSS

TOSS
THROW
SPLASH
FLOAT

HA!
RIGHT?!

I, FOR ONE, WILL NOT **TOLERATE** THIS ANY LONGER!

BONK!

HEY!

I'VE NEVER SWAM INSIDE THE HOUSE BEFORE!
BOUNCE
BUMP
SEE?
TOLD YA!
THIS IS GREAT!
SUCH AN AWESOME...
POOL PARTY!
SPLASH
SPLASH

NOW, KIDS... WE MUST SETTLE DOWN...
TOO MUCH FUN IS NOT...

AW...
MAYBE JUST A LITTLE BIT.

FFSSSSSH

HAH!

HAVING FUN, FISH?
IT STILL COUNTS.
EVEN BY ACCIDENT.

HUH? WHAT?
NO, I'M NOT!

FISH CAN'T HAVE FUN!

REALLY, FISH?
IT LOOKS LIKE YOU'RE HAVING FUN.
WELL, IT IS A GIANT FISHBOWL.

SPLASH
AW YEAH!
SPLASH
1
WOO-HOO!

SPLASH

SPLASH

BOUNCE
SPLASH

SWIM

CREAK

FALL
SPLOOSH

WHAT A MESS!
EVERYTHING IN THE HOUSE IS SOAKED!
WET, DAMP, AND WATERLOGGED!

HOW ARE WE GONNA CLEAN THIS UP?
MOM'S NOT GOING TO LIKE THIS WHEN SHE GETS HOME.

TUT-TUT, MY FRIEND.
I HAVE JUST THE THING.
OF COURSE YOU DO.
I KNEW YOU WOULD.

I PRESENT TO YOU...

REACH
SPLASH

...TA-DA!

WHOA!
WHAT IS THAT?

SPECIAL DEAL OF THE DAY!
THE SUPER SOAKY CLEAN MACHINE 3000!
IT'S SUPER!
IT'S SOAPY!
THE SUPER SOAKY CLEAN MACHINE 3000
IT CLEANS!
IT HAS EVERYTHING!
BUY IT NOW!*
*AVAILABLE FOR A LIMITED TIME ONLY IN YOUR IMAGINATION!

THE SUPER SOAKY CLEAN MACHINE 3000!
THE SUPER SOAKY CLEAN MACHINE 3000

WITH THING 1 AND THING 2 BEHIND THE OPERATIONS...
THE SUPER

PRESS
...WE ARE GUARANTEED TO MAKE ANY DIRTY JOB SQUEAKY CLEAN IN MOMENTS!

CHUGGA
CHUGGA
CHUGGA
CHUGGA
CHUG
THE

CHK
CHK
THE SUPER SOAKY CLEAN MACHINE 3000

CHUG
CHUG
SHAKE
BUBBS

POP
POP
POP
THIS CAN'T BE GOOD.
POP
PREPARE TO BE IMPRESSED.

WATCH THIS, FISH.
IT WILL CLEAN YOUR SOCKS OFF!
CLEAN MY WHAT?
I DON'T EVEN WEAR SOCKS.

OUR POOL PARTY JUST TURNED INTO A SUPER SUDSY CLEANING PARTY!

HERE!

GRAB A SCRUB BRUSH!

CATCH
CATCH
CATCH
CHUGGA
CHUG
THE SUPER SOAKY CLEAN MACHINE 3000
CHUG
CHUGGA
PRESS
OPEN

OPEN
BRUSH

BRUSH

MOP

SPONGE

BUCKET

SPRAY

CHUG
KAARKZ
ARMS
THE SUPER SOAKY CLEAN MACHINE 3000
SSRRKF

ISN'T IT BEAUTIFUL?
NOW LET'S SEE WHAT THE SUPER SOAKY CLEAN MACHINE 3000 CAN REALLY DO!

THE SUPER SOAKY CLEAN
HIT IT, THINGS!

PRESS

CLICK
CLICK
PULL
GEAR

SCRUB

SWOOSH

BRUSH
BRUSH
SCRUB
SCRUB

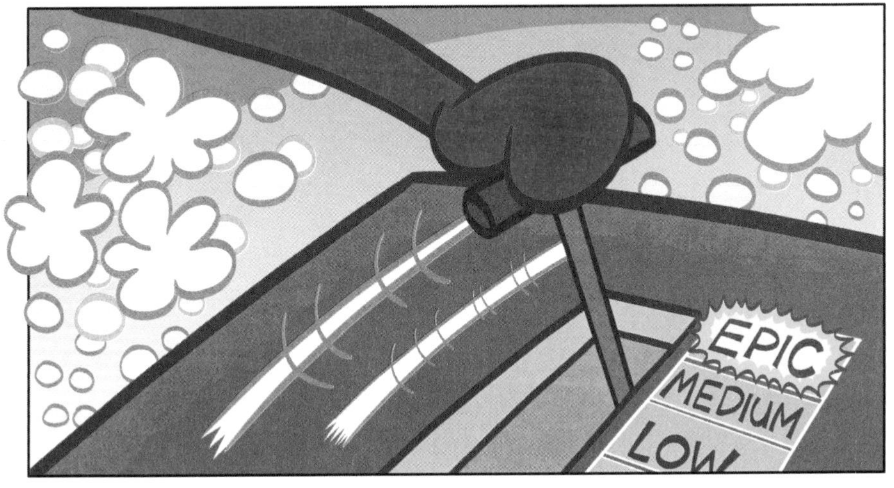
EPIC
MEDIUM
LOW

CHUG
CHUGGA
CHUG
CHUGGA
CHUG
CHUGGA

SWIM
SWIM
I NEVER SWAM IN BUBBLES BEFORE!
HA HA!
IT'S LIKE WE'RE FLOATING ON AIR!
BUBBLY FUN!

POP
POP

BLAH

PHWOO!

HA HA
HA HA
HA HA
HA

CHUGGA
CHUGGA
CHUGGA

RUMBLE
SHAKE
SHAKE
SHAKE

RUMBLE
BUMBLE

FFBOOMFF!!

SHOOF!
OKAY.
NOW WE'VE GONE TOO FAR!
AW.
FALL

THWNK!

PLOOP!

WHEW!

HEY!
IT'S ALL FUN AND GAMES...
...UNTIL THE FISH GOES FLYING THROUGH THE AIR!

ONCE AGAIN...
...GOOD JOB, THINGS!
THE SUPER SOAKY CLEAN MACHINE 3000
SOUNDS LIKE FISH IS HAVING A GREAT TIME.

HOW ABOUT YOU, KIDS?
THE HOUSE IS STILL SOGGY.
EVERYTHING IS VERY WET.
AND DAMP.
DON'T FORGET DAMP.

SIT TIGHT, MY FRIENDS.
I HAVE JUST THE THING.

LEAP
I KNEW YOU WERE GONNA...

WE SHOULD REALLY THINK ABOUT KEEPING THAT WINDOW CLOSED.

WHAT?

STRETCH

YOU'RE GONNA **LOVE** THIS...

PRESENTING...

*AVAILABLE FOR A LIMITED TIME ONLY IN YOUR IMAGINATION!

PRESENTING...
THE SUPER-DUPER BUBBLE SCOOPER!
IT'S REALLY JUST A **GIANT** BUBBLE VACUUM CLEANER!

HIT IT, THINGS!

PREP

START

VVMMMM

HA!
WOW!
IT'S VACUUMING UP ALL THE SUDS!

BUBBLE
BUBS
VVVRRMM
WHOA.
IT MIGHT BE WORKING TOO WELL!

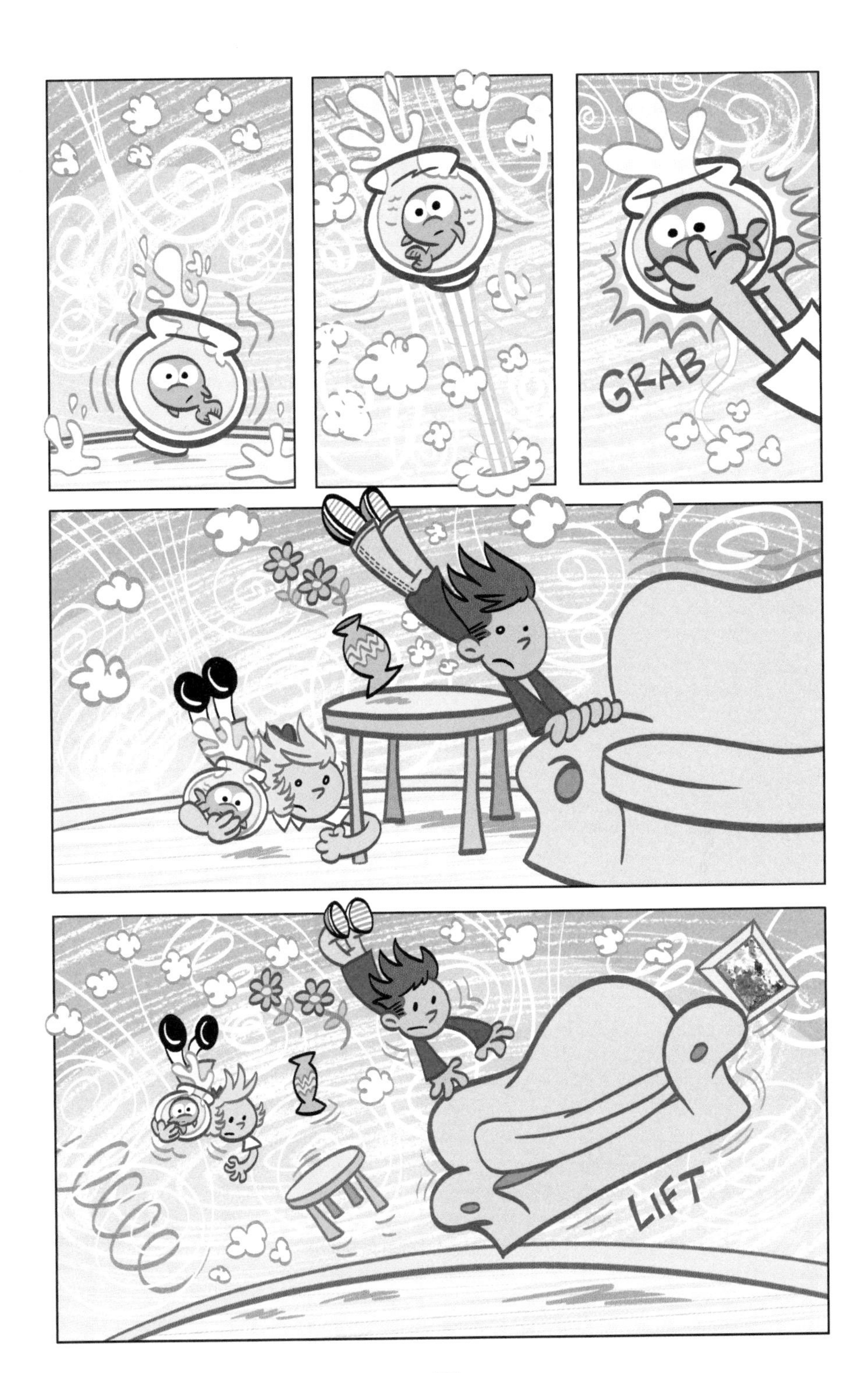
GRAB
LIFT

WOO-HOO!

SWIRL
WOOSH
SWIRL

STOP
FREEZE
STOP

FALL
FALL
FLOOR
LAND

RETRACT

THERE YOU GO!
ALL IS BACK TO NORMAL.
YOU'RE NO LONGER FISH!

LET'S HEAR IT! YAY, CAT!
hooray.

LOOKS LIKE YOU GOT A LITTLE SOMETHING RIGHT THERE.
BUFF
BUFF

PERFECT!

CLEAN AND SPARKLY, JUST LIKE NEW.

YOU ARE SO CLEAN, YOU DON'T NEED BATHS BEFORE BEDTIME.
REALLY?
NO BATHS?
SPEAKING OF BEDTIME...
IT'S GETTING LATE.
YOU BOTH HAVE SCHOOL IN THE MORNING.
RIGHT!
INHALE
WEE-OH-WEEEET!

POP
POP

OKAY, THING 1 AND THING 2...
OUR WORK IS DONE!

BACK IN THE BOX!

JUMP
HOP

SLAM!
OKAY!
GOTTA GO!
UNTIL NEXT TIME, KIDS!
MAYBE EVEN TOMORROW?
AFTER SCHOOL?
LATER.
SWOOP!
WAIT.
TOMORROW?
I THOUGHT THIS WAS OVER.

AT LEAST EVERYTHING IS CLEAN AGAIN.
SQUEAKY CLEAN!
FRESH.
AND JUST IN TIME FOR BED.

AW!
WE STILL NEED TO BRUSH OUR TEETH!
RACE YA.

WHAT A DAY.
ZIP!
RUN!
...DOES THIS BOWL SEEM SMALLER?

-GOOD NIGHT.

HOW TO DRAW
CAT IN THE HAT
CHARACTERS
1.
2.
3.
4.
5.
6.

HOW TO DRAW
CAT IN THE HAT
CHARACTERS
1.
2.
3.
4.
5.

HOW TO DRAW
CAT IN THE HAT
CHARACTERS
1.
2.
3.
4.
5.

HOW TO DRAW
CAT IN THE HAT
CHARACTERS
1.
2.
3.
4.
5.

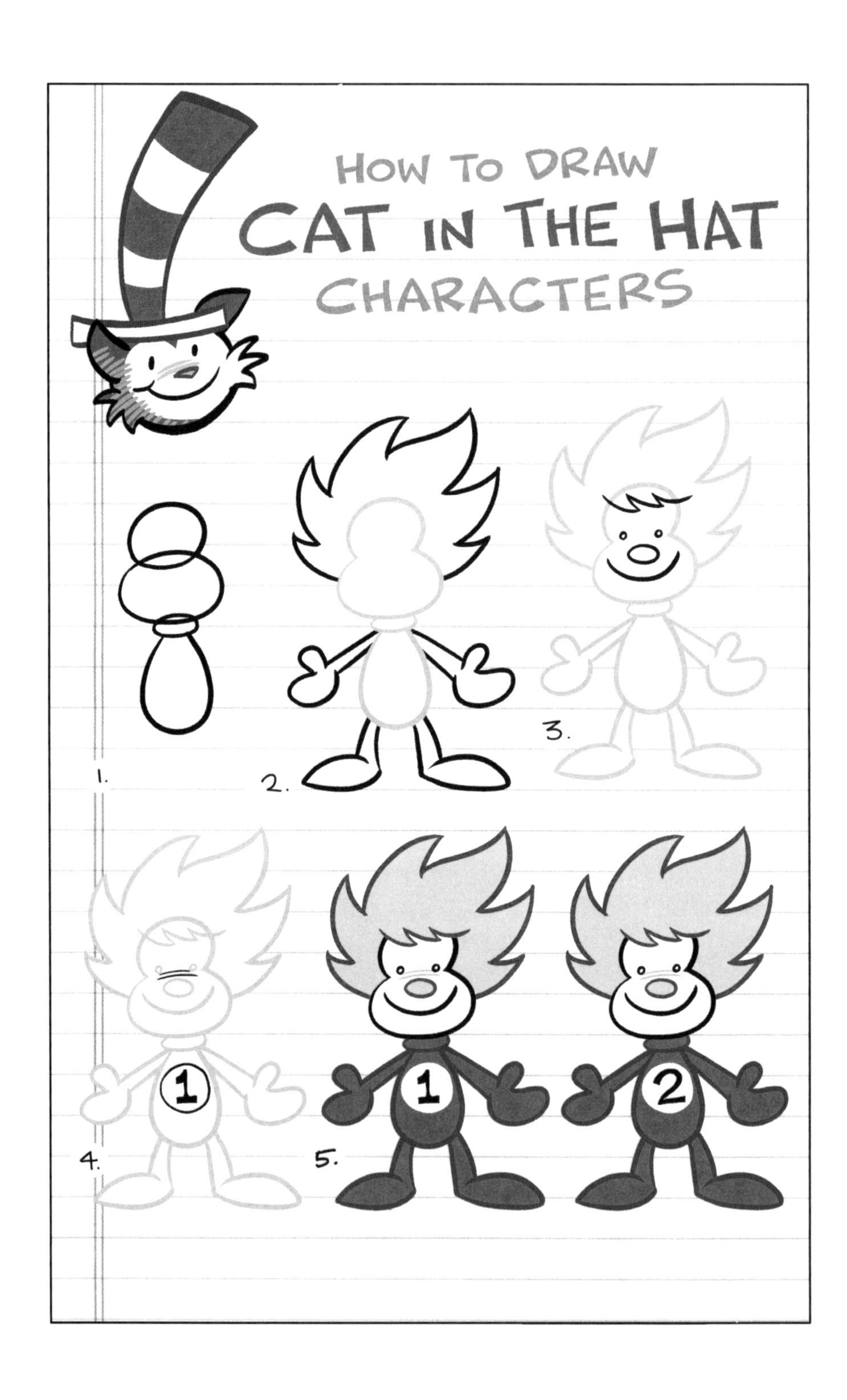
HOW TO DRAW
CAT IN THE HAT
CHARACTERS
1.
2.
3.
4.
1
5.
1
2

Art Baltazar is a super-cartoonist machine from the heart of Chicago! He's all about peace, love, and joy. He defines cartoons and comics not only as an art style but as a way of life. Art started his funky secret art studio in 1994 with his self-published comic book *The Cray-Baby Adventures.*

Art is part of the team behind the Eisner Award–winning Itty Bitty Hellboy and the *New York Times* bestselling and Eisner and Harvey Award–winning DC Comics' Tiny Titans. He is also the artist of the DC Super-Pets children's book series.

Art is the co-founder of the Aw Yeah Comics comic shop and co-creator of the Aw Yeah Comics! comic book series starring Action Cat and Adventure Bug. From small press to mainstream in a heartbeat—Art is living the dream! He stays home and draws comics and never has to leave the house! He lives with his lovely wife, Rose; sons, Sonny and Gordon; daughter, Audrey; and pup, Jingle Fett Baltazar!

AWESOME COMICS!
AWESOME KIDS!

Introduce your youngest reader to comics with

RH GRAPHIC

Learn more at RHCBooks.com

1617